Do Your Best, Tess!

Janet Morris Grimes
Illustrated by Jake Robbins

Copyright Notice

Do Your Best, Tess!

First edition. Copyright © 2022 by Janet Morris Grimes The information contained in this book is the intellectual property of Janet Morris Grimes and is governed by United States and International copyright laws. All rights reserved. No part of this publication, either text or image, may be used for any purpose other than personal use. Therefore, reproduction, modification, storage in a retrieval system, or retransmission, in any form or by any means, electronic, mechanical, or otherwise, for reasons other than personal use, except for brief quotations for reviews or articles and promotions, is strictly prohibited without prior written permission by the publisher.

This is a work of fiction. Names, characters, businesses, places, events, locales, and incidents are either the products of the author's imagination or used in a fictitious manner. Any resemblance to actual persons, living or dead, or actual events is purely coincidental.

Cover and Interior Design: Jake Robbins, Derinda Babcock

Editor(s): Derinda Babcock, Deb Haggerty

PUBLISHED BY: Elk Lake Publishing, Inc., 35 Dogwood Drive, Plymouth, MA 02360, 2022

Library Cataloging Data

Names: Grimes, Janet Morris (Janet Morris Grimes)

Do Your Best, Tess / Janet Grimes

50 p. 21.6 cm × 21.6 cm (8.5 in × 8.5 in.)

ISBN-13: 978-1-64949-639-3 (paperback) | 978-1-64949-640-9 (trade hardcover) | 978-1-64949-641-6 (trade paperback) | 978-1-64949-642-3 (e-book)

Key Words: children's social skills; children's character; children's manners and morals; children's virtues; children's values; children's learning disorders; parenting hyperactive children

Library of Congress Control Number: 2022941881 Fiction

Dedication

To my mother, who taught me to read, speak and write in a way that proved anything is possible.

To Lukas, Walker, Logan and Charlotte: may you each become the hero of your own story. I love you forever.

Tess was a busy little girl who preferred to spend each day doing everything but follow rules her parents tossed her way.

"Clean your room.
Hang your clothes.
Tie your shoes.
Comb your hair.
Go to school.
Feed the dog.
Go to bed.
Say your prayers."

"I'm so tired of choring, so I'll only try a little."

Come on, Tess.
Is that your best?
Can we help you with this riddle?

DO YOUR BEST, TESS!

DO YOUR BEST, TESS!

What Tess wanted most of all
was to become a star.
Could she sing at center stage?
Would her talent take her far?

Then, to her surprise,
the teacher said at noon,
"Time to hold auditions—
our school play opens soon."

"The moment I've been waiting for!
I'll try more than a little."

Come on, Tess.
Is that your best?
Can we help you with this riddle?

DO YOUR BEST, TESS!

DO YOUR BEST, TESS!

Tess sat down to learn her lines
but could not concentrate.
Then among a pile of clothes,
she found her roller skates.

With a 'woot' and a holler
she rattled down the street,
leaving the script on the floor,
her assignment incomplete.

Come on, Tess.
Is that your best?
Can we help you with this riddle?

DO YOUR BEST, TESS!

DO YOUR BEST, TESS!

In line for the auditions,
Tess hoped for a delay.
Since she forgot to practice,
she planned her getaway.

When the teacher called her name,
she turned away to flee.
"What if I'm not good enough
and my friends all laugh at me?"

"Is this what can happen when I only try a little?"

Come on, Tess.
Just do your best.
Can we help you with this riddle?

DO YOUR BEST, TESS!

DO YOUR BEST, TESS!

For the first time, Tess regretted
that she'd quit before she started.
If she'd done her very best,
she might not feel so brokenhearted.

Could Tess have learned to sing on stage
if she had followed through?
If she only had a second chance,
Tess would not quit too soon.

Come on, Tess.
Just do your best.
Can we help you with this riddle?

DO YOUR BEST, TESS!

DO YOUR BEST, TESS!

Tess pleaded with her teacher
to get another chance.
"I was too afraid to show you,
but I love to sing and dance."

Then Tess stepped in the spotlight
and belted out her song.
"I must confess. I did my best.
Why did I take so long?"

"Now that I know what best feels like, why did I try so little?"

You did it, Tess.
You did your best!
And we helped you with this riddle!

DO YOUR BEST, TESS!

DO YOUR BEST, TESS!

About the Author

Janet Morris Grimes may not have realized she was a writer at the time, but her earliest childhood memories were spent creating fairy-tale stories of the father she never knew. That desire to connect with the mysterious man in a treasured photograph gave her a deep love for the endless possibilities of a healing and everlasting story.

As a girl in the fourth grade, Janet Morris Grimes volunteered as a school library aid. Since that first day surrounded by those shelf-lined walls, she discovered characters that became her friends and stayed with her long after she closed the book. From that point on, she dreamed of writing stories that fill gaps in the hearts of her readers, like a good friend is supposed to do.

Contact Janet at janetmorrisgrimes.com

CPSIA information can be obtained
at www.ICGtesting.com
Printed in the USA
BVHW062339031222
653396BV00002B/24